Words by Keith Henry Brown &
National Book Award Winner Kathryn Erskine

Illustrated by
Keith Henry Brown

FARRAR STRAUS GIROUX
NEW YORK

RU
DMC

My dad is a DJ, and he always picks the best music—
tunes jivin', beat drivin', high-fivin'!

CHICK
COREA
SOLO PIANO
TOWN HALL
APRIL 10, 2014

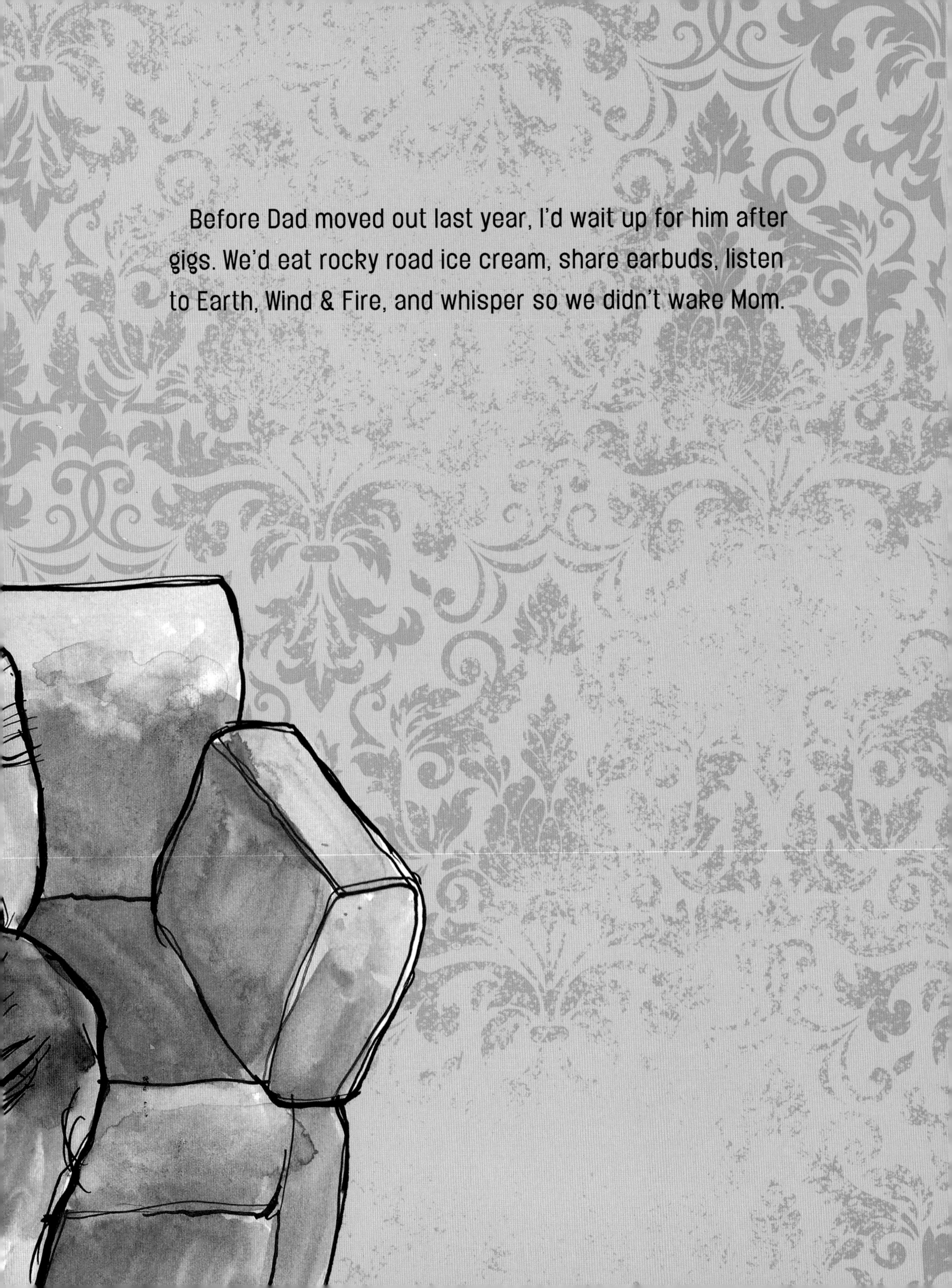

Before Dad moved out last year, I'd wait up for him after gigs. We'd eat rocky road ice cream, share earbuds, listen to Earth, Wind & Fire, and whisper so we didn't wake Mom.

After school, he'd shoot baskets with me and my friends.

I didn't even mind his dad jokes because everyone knows he's cool—he's DJ Dap Daddy!

He still dedicates a song to me on the radio at the end of his show: "Trevor, this is one of ours."

But lately, the pitch doesn't fit. I have my own music now.

It's been months, but eating rocky road alone or at his place feels out of sync.

Mom says, "You and your dad just need to find your new groove."

She's thinking about his new place.

I'm thinking about the new space between us.

MILES DAVIS

The end-of-school party is almost here, so Dad gets his old tunes ready to DJ, like he always does.

"You could play new covers or a remix—if you want," I say, a little offbeat.

"Change the classics? Nah, they're perfect the way they are."

We go to Mel's for dinner. Dad orders a grilled cheese for me every time because he thinks it's still my favorite.

"We could try a Cuban sandwich," I say, "like at Fernando's house."

"Who's Fernando?" he asks, and I realize he's never met my new friend. I don't tell him Fernando and I listen to our own music together.

When we play pickup near Dad's new place, I keep branching out, throwing three-pointers . . . mostly missing.

Dad says, "Stay inside the key, Trevor!"

That night, we do karaoke to Dad's old soul, but I don't feel much like singing.

"What's wrong?" Dad says.

"I think my voice is changing."

He laughs and gives me a hug. "You're too young for that."

Truth is, Dad thinks our music can stay the same. That we can stay the same. That *I* can stay the same. But next month is my birthday. I'll be a whole year older.

BIGGIE

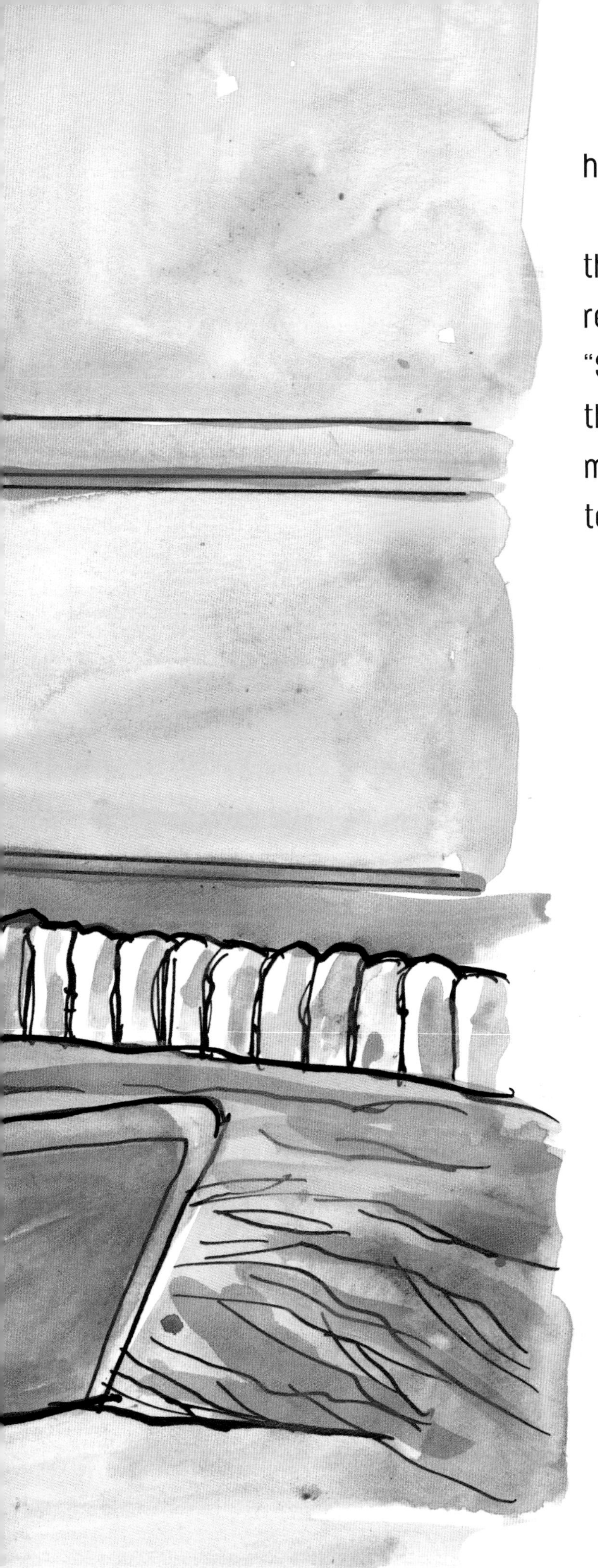

Mom tells me to talk to him. That he needs to hear who I am now.

So that night, when he says into the mic, “This is one of ours,” I really listen to the different parts of “Stand By Me.” I hear Dad humming the bass line in my head. I close my eyes and feel a more upbeat tempo . . . maybe a voice-over.

Pretty soon I'm picking out the best parts of Dad's favorites—a guitar solo here, backup singers there, some cool instruments—and sampling the best parts of *my* music, adding beatboxing, scratching, and vocals to make songs sound old and new at the same time.

It's the smoothness of Dad's voice with the zip of mine, the breath of his songs but the beat of mine.

The soul of Dad and the heart of me.

I surprise Dad with my new playlist before the party. I know my friends will be cool with it, but I really want him to like it too.

"You don't like our music anymore, Trevor?"

"It's still ours," I tell him. "Yours and mine."

He tries the first song, and just like I thought, kids start dancing, along with grown-ups. I used riffs from "It's the Same Old Song" with an up-tempo version of me and Stevie Wonder singing "I Just Called to Say I Love You."

Dad watches the crowd carefully, just like I'm watching him.

His shoulders start moving to one of my favorite dance tracks merging into a fast version of "We Are Family." When he plays my remix of "Celebration," he's practically hoppin'. As my mash-up of "Stand By Me" plays, he calls me up to the stage.

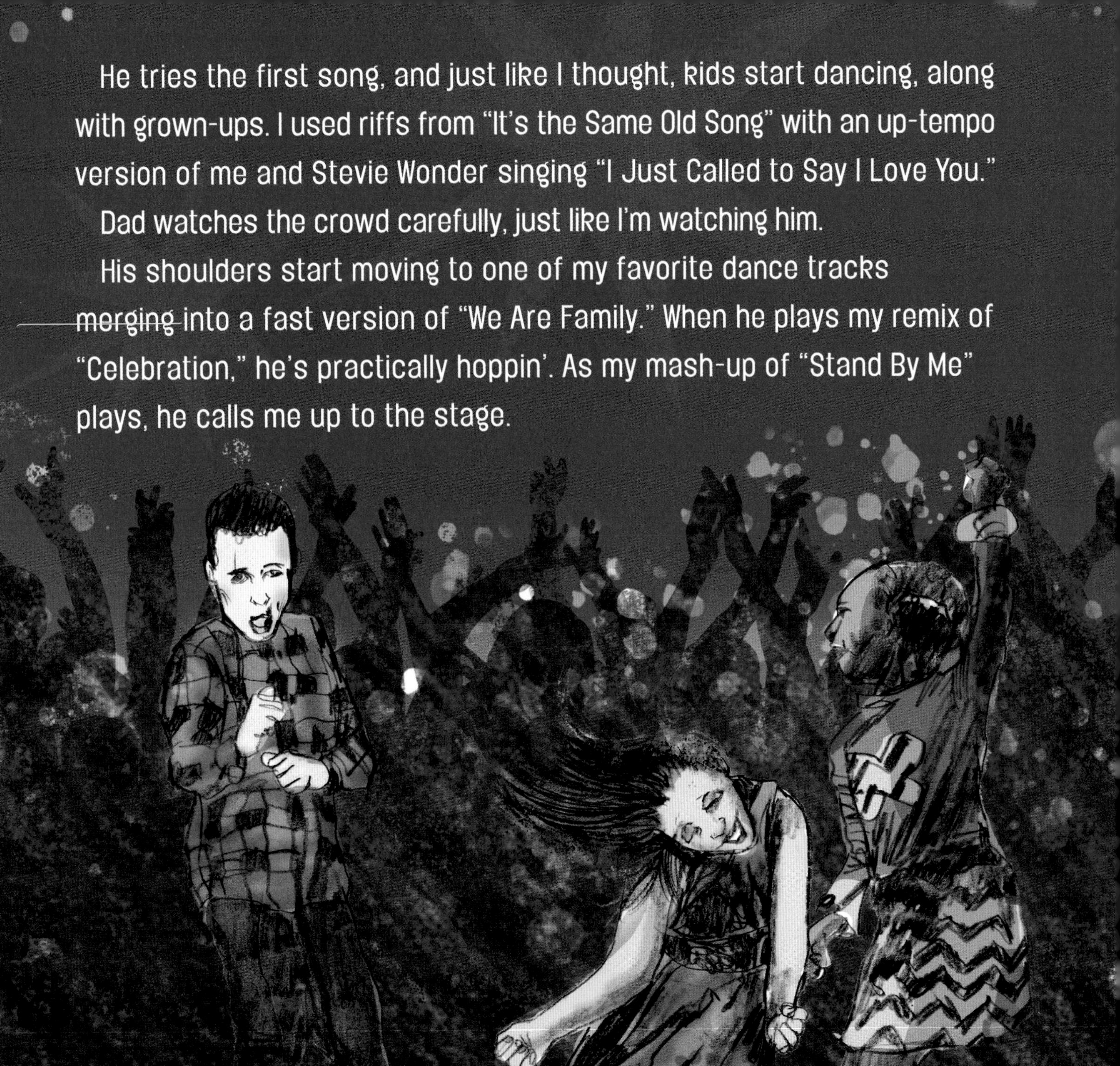

"I like your new music, Trevor," he says with a smile.

"*Our* new music," I tell him.

It's my first time ever DJing with Dad—hip-hoppin', beat boppin', tunes poppin', not stoppin'!

When Dad and I finally take a break, the rocky road ice cream goes down smooth. Bring on summer!

Now Dad sees who I am
We got new tunes, and we can jam

Taking turns sampling everything
Mix it up, mash it up, make it sing

Growing a space where we both belong
Finding our rhythm and making our song

Doo-wop, go-go, wonky, slap
Bebop, boogie-woogie, boom boom bap!

To all those magnificent single women who brought up all these fine boys to be extraordinary men —K.H.B.

To kids whose families change: Your folks still love you. That part never changes. —K.E.

Farrar Straus Giroux Books for Young Readers
An imprint of Macmillan Publishing Group, LLC
120 Broadway, New York, NY 10271 • mackids.com

Our books may be purchased in bulk for promotional, educational, or business use. Please contact your local bookseller or the Macmillan Corporate and Premium Sales Department at (800) 221-7945 ext. 5442 or by email at MacmillanSpecialMarkets@macmillan.com.

Library of Congress Cataloging-in-Publication Data is available.

First edition, 2023
Book design by Marissa Asuncion
Color separations by Embassy Graphics
Printed in China by Hung Hing Off-set Printing Co. Ltd., Heshan City, Guangdong Province

ISBN 978-0-374-30742-4 (hardcover)
1 3 5 7 9 10 8 6 4 2

The illustrations for this book were created mostly using ink, pencil, and watercolor with Photoshop added. The text was set in Elephant. Art direction by Aram Kim and Jen Keenan. Production was supervised by Allene Cassagnol and Susan Doran, and the production editor was Helen Seachrist. Edited by Grace Kendall, with support from Asia Harden and Elizabeth Lee.